JANE AUSTEN'S
LITTLE ADVICE
BOOK

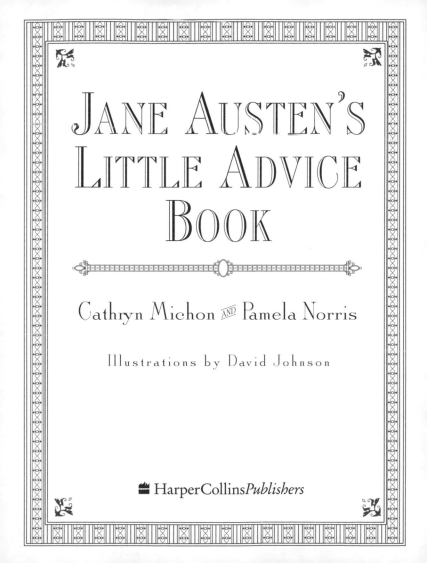

JANE AUSTEN'S LITTLE ADVICE BOOK

Cathryn Michon *AND* Pamela Norris

Illustrations by David Johnson

■ HarperCollins*Publishers*

HarperCollins books may be purchased for educational, business, or sales promotional use. For information please write: Special Markets Department, HarperCollins Publishers, Inc., 10 East 53rd Street, New York, NY 10022.

FIRST EDITION

Designed by Joel Avirom & Jason Snyder

Library of Congress Cataloging-in-Publication Data
Austen, Jane, 1775–1817.
    Jane Austen's little advice book / Cathryn Michon and Pamela Norris.
        p.   cm.
    Selected quotations from Jane Austen's works topically arranged by the editors.
    ISBN 0-06-018707-7
    1. Austen, Jane, 1775–1817—Quotations. 2. Conduct of life—Quotations,
maxims, etc. 3. Quotations, English. I. Michon, Cathryn. II. Norris, Pamela.
III. Title.
PR4032.M53   1996
823' .7—dc20   96-8432

96 97 98 99 00 ❖/ HC 10 9 8 7 6 5 4 3 2 1

To Eric and Paul

Only two critical notices of Jane Austen's *Sense and Sensibility* appeared in her lifetime, although both were favorable. This review appeared in the *British Critic* in May 1812; the author is anonymous.

"We . . . assure (our readers), that they may peruse these volumes not only with satisfaction, but with real benefits, for they may learn from them, if they please, many sober and salutary maxims for the conduct of life, exemplified in a very pleasing and entertaining narrative."

In other words, not only are these books great, but they're full of really good advice. That was the premise upon which we started this project, but we were surprised to find that someone basically had the same idea a hundred and eighty-four years ago. Perhaps this proves that a good idea is always a good idea, but sometimes you need a big movie to push it through.

So for everyone who thinks this book was rushed out to take advantage of the Jane Austen craze, we say: Hey. It was almost two hundred years in the making.

— *C.S.M. AND P.R.N.*

AUTHORS' THANKS

The enthusiasm of Maria Hjelm made this entire project possible.

We would like to thank Carole Bidnick and Jane Dystel for all their help, advice and support. Thanks also to Diane Reverand, Meaghan Dowling, Nellie Diaz, Megan Barber, Ileen Getz, Ted Michon II, Tom and Nancy Norris, and Ted and Evie Michon. Finally, for their patience, thanks to Juliet and Carolina Jane.

CONTENTS

CONTENTS

INTRODUCTION

Facts are such horrid things!

—LADY SUSAN

Who is Jane Austen? She was a woman who wrote almost exclusively about courtship and marriage, but who never married. She was a daughter who spent her life primarily in the company of her family, most of whom seemed unaware, if not actually dismissive of, her talent. She was the author of novels so beloved that they remain popular nearly two hundred years after her death, yet while she lived, she had to pay to have them published. She is now perhaps the most famous female writer who ever lived, yet her gravestone at Winchester Cathedral initially did not mention that she was an author at all. It was nearly fifty years after her death when an additional brass tablet was installed nearby, informing people of this small fact.

But the greatest paradox of Jane Austen may be that her image (which seems to be that of bonnets and crinolines, tea and gentility) is sometimes completely at odds with her writings, which are always sly, often biting, and sometimes actually vicious . . . in an extremely entertaining way.

For those who have never read her works, this book is meant to be an introduction to Jane Austen; for those who know her novels, it is meant to be an enjoyable rediscovery of their wit and insight. This is not a scholarly work, nor is it likely to be mistaken for one. The facts of Jane Austen's life are not always clear, and the scholarly works have a tendency to contradict one another. The biographical details cited herein are the more thoroughly documented ones.

Some quotations in this book have been taken from Jane Austen's own mouth (via her letters) and some from the mouths of her characters, not all of whom, of course, are expressing Miss Austen's exact sentiments. Vagaries of spelling and punctuation have been changed in order to avoid the distracting use of *sic*. And sometimes we take something totally out of context to make a joke. Serious students of Jane Austen: you have been warned.

The sudden and massive revival of interest in Miss Austen's works has been explained in any number of ways. The real answer is probably very simple: her writing is wonderful. Rather than dissect her appeal yet again, we prefer to let her words stand for themselves.

—THE AUTHORS

MEN & WOMEN

If there is anything disagreeable going on,
men are always sure to get out of it.

PERSUASION

Jane Austen's great topic was the battle of the sexes. All her novels are about the search for the right person to marry. Apparently, this was no easier in the early nineteenth century than it is today. It seems deeply unfair that Jane's heroines always finally found the man who appreciated their lively minds, but Jane herself never did.

There is no doubt that Jane was a feminist. She also loved men and she particularly loved to make fun of them. For example:

> I meant to be uncommonly clever in taking so decided a dislike to him, without any reason. It is such a spur to one's genius, such an opening for wit, to have a dislike of that kind. One may be continually abusive without saying anything just; but one cannot always be laughing at a man without now and then stumbling on something witty.

PRIDE AND PREJUDICE

But lest she be accused of male-bashing, it should also be noted Jane often bashed her own sex as well:

> (She) is like any other short girl with a broad nose and wide mouth, fashionable dress and exposed bosom.

NORTHANGER ABBEY

THE SEXES

On Playing Dumb

A woman especially, if she have the misfortune of knowing anything, should conceal it as well as she can.

NORTHANGER ABBEY

On Why Men and Women are Equally Good

In every power, of which taste is the foundation, excellence is pretty fairly divided among the sexes.

NORTHANGER ABBEY

On the Mall vs. Football

One half the world cannot understand the pleasures of the other.

EMMA

On Why Women Are Twice as Good as Men

. . . no one can think more highly of the understanding of women than I do. In my opinion, nature has given them so much, that they never find it necessary to use more than half.

NORTHANGER ABBEY

MEN... GOOD

On the Ideal Man

All I want in a man is someone who rides bravely, dances beautifully, sings with vigor, reads passionately, and whose taste agrees in every point with my own.

SENSE AND SENSIBILITY

On More Requirements for the Ideal Man

He is just what a young man ought to be . . . sensible, good humored, lively; and I never saw such happy manners . . . He is also handsome . . . which a young man ought likewise to be, if he possibly can.

PRIDE AND PREJUDICE

On the Importance of Finding the Ideal Man

I could not be happy with a man whose taste did not in every point coincide with my own. He must enter into all my feelings; the same books, the same music must charm us both.

SENSE AND SENSIBILITY

...AND BAD

On Infuriating Men

What can you have to do with hearts? You men have none of you any hearts.

NORTHANGER ABBEY

On Men Who Can't Shut Up

He begged pardon for having displeased her. In a softened tone she declared herself not at all offended; but he continued to apologize for about a quarter of an hour.

PRIDE AND PREJUDICE

5

On Stupid Men

I am going tomorrow where I shall find a man who has not one agreeable quality, who has neither manner nor sense to recommend him. Stupid men are the only ones worth knowing, after all.

PRIDE AND PREJUDICE

On Boring Men

(She) was doomed to the repeated details of his day's sport, good or bad, his boast of his dogs, his jealousy of his neighbors, his doubts on their qualifications, and his zeal after poachers, subjects which will not find their way to female feelings without some talent on one side or some attachment on the other . . .

MANSFIELD PARK

On Men Not Being That Big of a Deal

What are men to rocks and mountains?

PRIDE AND PREJUDICE

WOMEN... GOOD

On a Woman Who Never Speaks Unless She Has Something to Say

She was not a woman of many words, for unlike people in general, she proportioned them to the number of her ideas.

SENSE AND SENSIBILITY

On the Need for Great Women

Every neighborhood should have a great lady.

SANDITON

On Women's Loyalty

All the privilege I claim for my own sex . . . is that of loving longest, when existence or when hope is gone.

PERSUASION

On the Enduring Charms of Bimbos

(She was) a good humored girl, but as empty headed as himself, had nothing to say that could be worth hearing, and (was) listened to with as much delight as the rattle of the chaise.

PRIDE AND PREJUDICE

On a Womanly Charm That Never Fails

The sudden acquisition of ten thousand pounds was the most remarkable charm of the young lady to whom he was now rendering himself agreeable.

PRIDE AND PREJUDICE

8

...AND BAD

On Golddiggers

(They are) very accomplished and ignorant . . . the object of all they do being to captivate some man of much better fortune than their own.

SANDITON

On Drama Queens

A young lady who faints must be recovered; questions must be answered, and surprises explained. Such events are very interesting; but the suspense of them cannot last long.

PRIDE AND PREJUDICE

On Women Who Believe Anything

. . . that woman is fool indeed, who while insulted by accusation, can be worked on by compliments.

LADY SUSAN

9

On Foolish Women

Oh! What a silly thing is woman! How vain, how unreasonable! To suppose that a young man would be seriously attached in the course of four and twenty hours to a girl who has nothing to recommend her but a good pair of eyes.

THE JUVENILIA OF JANE AUSTEN

On Certain Women

. . . (she) was one of that numerous class of females, whose society can raise no other emotion than surprise at there being any men in the world who could like them well enough to marry them.

NORTHANGER ABBEY

OLD BOYFRIENDS
—

On the Attractiveness of Men You've Broken Up With

She became jealous of his esteem, when she could no longer hope to be benefited by it. She wanted to hear of him, when there seemed the least chance of gaining intelligence. She was convinced that she could have been happy with him, when it was no longer likely that they should meet.

PRIDE AND PREJUDICE

On Being Afraid of Creamy White Envelopes

Why should you be living in dread of his marrying somebody else? Yet how natural!

THE LETTERS OF
JANE AUSTEN

*On Discovering the Happy
Engagement of a
Former Beau*

All I can say is that if it is true, he has used a young lady of my acquaintance abominably ill, and I wish him with all my soul his wife may plague his heart out.

SENSE AND SENSIBILITY

On Rewriting One's Own History

Perhaps I did not always love him so well as I do now. But in such cases as these a good memory is unpardonable.

PRIDE AND PREJUDICE

On the Best Way to Get Over a Man

She consoled herself for the loss of her husband by considering that she could do very well without him.

MANSFIELD PARK

FEMINISM

—

On the Dearth of Women Writers

Men have had every advantage in telling us their own story. Education has been theirs in so much higher a degree; the pen has been in their hands.

PERSUASION

On the Way Men Write About Women . . .

I do not think I ever opened a book in my life which had
not something to say upon a woman's inconstancy. Songs
and proverbs all talk of woman's fickleness. But perhaps
you will say, these were all written by men.

PERSUASION

. . . And the Absence of Women in History Books

Real solemn history, I cannot be interested . . . The
quarrels of popes and kings, with wars or pestilences in
every page; the men all so good for nothing and hardly
any women at all.

HISTORY OF ENGLAND

On the Enduring Double Standard

. . . loss of virtue in a female is irretrievable . . . one false
step involves her in endless ruin . . . her reputation is no
less brittle than it is beautiful . . . she cannot be too much
guarded in her behavior towards the undeserving of the
other sex.

PRIDE AND PREJUDICE

On Why Men Are from Mars and Women Are from Venus

(Women's feelings) are the most tender. Man is more robust than woman, but he is not longer-lived; which exactly explains my view of the nature of their attachments . . . You are always laboring and toiling; exposed to every risk and hardship . . . It would be too hard indeed . . . if woman's feelings were to be added to all this.

PERSUASION

14

LOVE & MARRIAGE

It is a truth universally acknowledged, that a single man in possession of a good fortune must be in want of a wife.
—PRIDE AND PREJUDICE

Jane Austen never married. This, however, does not mean that she was never asked, that she was irretrievably plain, or that she was never in love. One acquaintance recalled her as "the prettiest, silliest, most affected, husband-hunting butterfly" in her memory. Her niece Caroline Austen wrote that Jane's "was the first face I can remember thinking pretty".

The only love affair of Jane's that is known was with the handsome Irishman Tom Lefroy. She wrote ironically of their innocent flirtation: "I am almost afraid to tell you how my Irish friend and I behaved. Imagine to yourself everything most profligate and shocking in the way of dancing and sitting down together." The affair went nowhere, however, allegedly because neither Jane nor Tom had any money.

Upper- and middle-class marriage in Jane's time was a serious business, more like a corporate merger than a romantic folly. Pre-nuptial agreements were the rule, and you could be sued for breaking an engagement. Jane was actually engaged one time, to the son of family friends. He was twenty-one; she was nearly twenty-seven and considered ancient. There seems to have been no particular affec-

tion on either side, and the day after Jane accepted the pro-
posal, she changed her mind and refused. This caused a
huge brouhaha in both families, but Jane stood her ground.
The man's name, incidentally, was Harris Bigg-Wither,
which you would think reason enough not to marry him.

LOVE

On "It's Either Love or Chronic Fatigue Syndrome"

This sensation of listlessness, weariness, stupidity, this
disinclination to sit down and employ myself, this feeling
of everything's being dull and insipid about the house! I
must be in love.

EMMA

On Love as Something to Avoid

Preserve yourself from first love . . . and you need not fear
a second.

THE JUVENILIA OF JANE AUSTEN

On Love as Something to Seize

No one can ever be in love more than once in their life.

SENSE AND SENSIBILITY

On Love as Addiction

The mere habit of learning to love is the thing, and a teachableness of disposition in a young lady is a great blessing.

NORTHANGER ABBEY

On Love as Fatal Attraction

Oh! when there is so much love on one side, there is no occasion for it on the other.

THE JUVENILIA OF JANE AUSTEN

On Love as Boy Craziness

I am always in love with every handsome man in the world.

THE JUVENILIA OF JANE AUSTEN

18

On Love as Just Plain Craziness

There is nothing people are so often deceived in, as the state of their own affections.

NORTHANGER ABBEY

On the Inevitability of Love

. . . he is so very much preoccupied by the idea of not being in love with her, that I should not wonder if it were to end in his being so at last.

THE JUVENILIA OF JANE AUSTEN

On the Pain of Love

Poor fellow! He is quite distracted by jealousy, which I am not very sorry for, as I know no better support of love.

LADY SUSAN

On Loving Someone for Their Good Taste

I must confess that his affection originated in nothing better than gratitude . . . a persuasion of her partiality for him had been the only excuse of giving her a serious thought.

NORTHANGER ABBEY

PASSION

—

On Having a Passionate Nature

I have no notion of loving people by halves . . . My attachments are always excessively strong . . . I believe my feelings are stronger than anybody's; I am sure they are too strong for my own peace.

NORTHANGER ABBEY

On Passion Not Being Everything

How little of permanent happiness could belong to a couple who were only brought together because their passions were stronger than their virtue.

PRIDE AND PREJUDICE

On Passion Being Everything After All

Still, however, she had enough to feel! It was agitation, pain, pleasure, a something between delight and misery.

PERSUASION

On Finding Passion When You Least Expect It

She had been forced into prudence in her youth, she
learned romance as she grew older—the natural sequence
of an unnatural beginning.

PERSUASION

COURTSHIP

—

*On Predicting the Dismal Dating Climate for Single Women
in New York*

There was a scarcity of men in general, and a still greater
scarcity of any that were good for much.

LETTER TO HER SISTER CASSANDRA

On the Remote Odds of Finding the Ideal Man

The more I know of the world, the more I am convinced
that I shall never see a man whom I can really love. I
require so much!

SENSE AND SENSIBILITY

On Why the Right Man Never Seems to Call

. . . all have believed themselves to be in danger from the pursuit of some one whom they wished to avoid; and all have been anxious for the attentions of some one whom they wished to please.

NORTHANGER ABBEY

On a Blind Date

He is undoubtedly remarkably plain; but that is nothing compared with his entire want of gentility. I had no right to expect much, and I did not expect much, but I had no idea that he could be so very clownish, so totally without air. I had imagined him, I confess, a degree or two nearer gentility.

EMMA

On Simplifying the Love Process

To be fond of dancing was a certain step towards falling in love.

PRIDE AND PREJUDICE

On the Romantic Effects of a Sea Breeze

They must all go to Brighton. That is the place to get husbands.

PRIDE AND PREJUDICE

On Not Playing Hard to Get

If a woman conceals her affection . . . from the object of it, she may lose the opportunity of fixing him . . . In nine cases out of ten, a woman had better show more affection than she feels.

PRIDE AND PREJUDICE

On Lowered Expectations

I think I could like any good humored man with a comfortable income.

THE WATSONS

On the Difficulty of Fulfilling Those Lowered Expectations

> But there certainly are not so many men of large fortune in the world as there are pretty women to deserve them.

MANSFIELD PARK

On Meeting Mr. Right

> I like this man; pray heaven no harm come of it!

LADY SUSAN

On One of the Ten Stupid Things Women Do to Mess Up Their Lives

> A lady's imagination is very rapid; it jumps from admiration to love, from love to matrimony, in a moment.

PRIDE AND PREJUDICE

On Why Lovers Need to Be in the Same Area Code

> . . . with lovers . . . no subject is finished, no communication is even made, till it has been made at least twenty times over.

SENSE AND SENSIBILITY

On Loving the Torture of Romance

Next to being married, a girl likes to be crossed in love a little now and then. It is something to think of, and gives her a sort of distinction among her companions,

PRIDE AND PREJUDICE

On Men Being Impossible to Figure Out

If he fears me, why come hither? If he no longer cares for me, why silent? Teasing, teasing man! I will think no more about him..

PRIDE AND PREJUDICE

25

On Who's Tricking Whom

Women fancy admiration means more than it does. And men take care that they should.

PRIDE AND PREJUDICE

On Men Who Can't Commit

You may like him well enough to marry, but not well enough to wait.

LETTER TO HER NIECE FANNY

On Drama Kings

This man is almost too gallant to be in love . . . but I suppose there may be a hundred different ways of being in love . . . but he does sigh and languish and study for compliments rather more than I could endure as a principal.

EMMA

On Not Being a Tease

I have no pretensions whatever to that kind of elegance which consists in tormenting a respectable man.

PRIDE AND PREJUDICE

26

On Ignorance as Bliss

Where people wish to attach, they should always be ignorant. To come with a well-informed mind, is to come with an inability of administering to the vanity of others, which a sensible person would always wish to avoid.

NORTHANGER ABBEY

On Knowing That an Affair Is Winding Down . . .

. . . it is therefore most probable that our indifference will soon be mutual, unless his regard, which appeared to spring from knowing nothing of me at first, is best supported by never seeing me.

LETTER TO HER SISTER CASSANDRA

. . . And What to Tell Your Girlfriend When It Is

Have you no comforts? No friends? Is your loss such as leaves no opening for consolation? Much as you suffer now, think of what you would have suffered if the discovery of his character had been delayed to a later period, if your engagement had been carried on for months and months, as it might have been, before he chose to put an end to it. Every additional day of unhappy confidence on your side would have made the blow more dreadful.

SENSE AND SENSIBILITY

On Ladies' Men

With men he can be rational and unaffected, but when he has ladies to please, every feature works.

EMMA

27

On the Erotic Appeal of Bad Manners

Is not general incivility the very essence of love?

PRIDE AND PREJUDICE

On the Wisdom of Ignoring the Advice "Give it Time"

Seven years would be insufficient to make some people acquainted with each other, and seven days are more than enough for others.

SENSE AND SENSIBILITY

On Being Realistic

There are such beings in the world perhaps, one in a thousand, as the creature you and I should think perfection, where grace and spirit are united to worth, where manners are equal to the heart and understanding, but such a person may not come your way, or if he does, he may not be the eldest son of a man of fortune, the brother of your particular friend, and belonging to your own country.

LETTER TO HER NIECE FANNY

On an Impossible Man Finding a Willing Woman

. . . his friends may well rejoice in his having met with one of the very few sensible women who would have accepted him, or have made him happy if they had

PRIDE AND PREJUDICE

PROPOSALS
—

On the Eternal Arrogance of Men

. . . it is always incomprehensible to a man that a woman should ever refuse an offer of marriage. A man always imagines a woman to be ready for anybody who asks her.

EMMA

On How a Proposal Perks You Up

An engaged woman is always more agreeable than a dis-engaged. She is satisfied with herself. Her cares are over, and she feels that she may exert all her powers of pleasing without suspicion. All is safe with a lady engaged; no harm can be done.

MANSFIELD PARK

On Being Absolutely Sure That What You Thought Was a
Proposal Actually Was One . . .

Did not you misunderstand him? You were both talking
of other things; of business, shows of cattle, or new
drills—and might not you, in the confusion of so many
subjects, mistake him? It was not (her) hand that he was
certain of—it was the dimensions of some famous ox.

EMMA

And Being Sure How to Answer

If a woman doubt as to whether she should accept a man
or not, she certainly ought to refuse him. If she can hesi-
tate as to "Yes," she ought to say "No" directly. It is not a
state to be safely entered into with doubtful feelings, with
half a heart.

EMMA

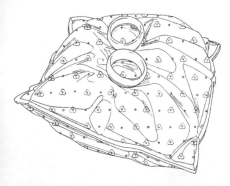

WEDDINGS

On the Importance of Making the Papers

I have not seen it in the papers. And one may as well be single, if the wedding is not to be in print.

LETTER TO HER NIECE ANNA

On the Joy of Being Always a Bridesmaid and Never a Bride

I never wish to act a more principal part at a wedding than superintending and directing the dinner, and therefore while I can get any of my acquaintance to marry for me, I shall never think of doing it myself.

THE JUVENILIA OF JANE AUSTEN

. . . But the Bride Still Rules

A bride, you know, my dear, is always the first in company, let the others be who they may.

EMMA

31

MARRIAGE
—

On Marriage

It is a truth universally acknowledged, that a single man in possession of a good fortune, must be in want of a wife.

PRIDE AND PREJUDICE

On Honesty in Marriage

. . . of all transactions, the one which people expect most from others, and are least honest themselves.

MANSFIELD PARK

On Happiness in Marriage

Happiness in marriage is entirely a matter of chance . . . it is better to know as little as possible of the defects of the person with whom you are to pass your life.

PRIDE AND PREJUDICE

On Those Who Are Against Marriage

I pay very little regard . . . to what any young person says
on the subject of marriage. If they profess a disinclination
for it, I only set it down that they have not seen the right
person.

MANSFIELD PARK

On Marrying for Love

I consider everybody as having a right to marry once in
their lives for love, if they can.

LETTER TO HER SISTER CASSANDRA

On Marrying for Other Reasons

. . . there are not many in my rank of life who can afford
to marry without some attentions to money.

PRIDE AND PREJUDICE

On Marrying for the Worst Reasons

She was complete: being prepared for matrimony by a hatred of home, restraint, and tranquillity; by the misery of disappointed affection, and contempt of the man she was to marry.

MANSFIELD PARK

. . . And for the Best Reasons

And now . . . having written so much on one side of the question, I shall turn round and entreat you not to commit yourself farther, and not to think of accepting him, unless you really do like him.

THE LETTERS OF JANE AUSTEN

On the Downside of Marrying an Old Guy

. . . of what a mistake were you guilty in marrying a man of his age! Just old enough to be formal, ungovernable, and to have the gout—too old to be agreeable, and too young to die.

LADY SUSAN

34

. . . And the Upside

(She) is so much pleased with the state of widowhood as
to be going to put in for being a widow again.

LETTER TO CASSANDRA

On the Secret Language of Love

Husbands and wives generally understand when opposition will be in vain.

PERSUASION

SPINSTERHOOD

On Marriage Perhaps Not Being All That It's Cracked Up to Be

I think that the pleasantest part of . . . married life must
be the dinners, the breakfasts, and luncheons, and bil-
liards . . .

LETTER TO HER BROTHER FRANK

On the Real Problem with Spinsterhood

A single woman with a narrow income must be a ridiculous, disagreeable old maid, the proper sport of boys and girls; but a single woman of good fortune is always respectable, and may be a sensible and pleasant as anybody else.

EMMA

On a Bad Day Job Beating a Bad Marriage

To be so bent on marriage—to pursue a man merely for the sake of a situation—is the sort of thing that shocks me; I cannot understand it. Poverty is a great evil, but to a woman of education and feeling it ought not, it cannot be the greatest. I would rather be a teacher at a school (and I can think of nothing worse) than marry a man I did not like.

LADY SUSAN

On the Ideal Single Life

I could do very well single for my own part. A little company, and a pleasant ball now and then, would be enough for me, if one could be young forever . . .

THE WATSONS

. . . And the Real Single Life

Single women have a dreadful propensity for being poor—which is one very strong argument in favor of matrimony.

LETTER TO
HER NIECE FANNY

LOVE & MARRIAGE

FAMILY

A family of ten children will always be called a fine family,
where there are heads and arms and legs enough for the number.
NORTHANGER ABBEY

Jane Austen spent most of her life in the company of her large and close family. She was the youngest daughter in a family of seven children, five sons and two daughters. They were all enthusiastic readers. The family also put on plays in their barn, which makes them sound like an old Mickey Rooney/Judy Garland movie, but in the days before VCR's, you had to do something in the evenings.

Her father was a gentleman farmer and the rector of Steventon. He sent both Jane and her older sister Cassandra to boarding school, at some financial sacrifice to himself, at a time when such an education for mere women was considered unnecessary . . . something for which Jane's readers can thank him. Her mother is generally remembered as a little flighty, a bit of a hypochondriac, and certainly no fan of Jane's satire, which, funnily enough, is often directed at mothers.

Jane's sister Cassandra was her close and lifelong companion. "If Cassandra were going to have her head cut off, Jane would insist on sharing her fate" was how their mother put it. Cassandra and Jane actually did share the early-nineteenth-century version of the Fate Worse than Death, namely, spinsterhood.

FAMILY

On Why You Keep Your Mouth Shut at Thanksgiving

Even the smooth surface of family union seems worth
preserving, though there may be nothing durable
beneath.

PERSUASION

. . . And Why There's Always Someone Who Doesn't

There is someone in most families privileged by superior
abilities of spirits to say anything.

SANDITON

. . . And on Loving Your Family Anyway

(She had) . . . too much good sense to be proud of her
family, and too much good nature to live at variance with
anyone.

LADY SUSAN

MOTHERS

—

On Mothers Being Easily Deluded

> . . . a fond mother . . . in pursuit of praise for her children
> . . . (is) the most rapacious of human beings . . . and the
> most credulous . . . she will swallow anything.

SENSE AND SENSIBILITY

On Being Embarrassed by One's Mother

> My mother means well, but she does not know—no one
> can know—how much I suffer from what she says.

PRIDE AND PREJUDICE

FATHERS

—

On "Dad's Approval" as the Kiss of Death

> The very circumstance of his being her father's choice,
> too, was so much in his disfavor . . . yet that of itself ought
> to have been sufficient reason in (her eyes) . . . for reject-
> ing him.

THE JUVENILIA OF JANE AUSTEN

SISTERS

On Why You Need to Talk to Your Sister

> But we must stem the tide of malice, and pour into the wounded bosoms of each other, the balm of sisterly consolation.

PRIDE AND PREJUDICE

. . . And When You Never Listen to Her

> I have never yet found that the advice of a sister could prevent a young man's being in love if he chose it.

LADY SUSAN

BROTHERS

—

On Brotherly Conversations

What strange creatures brothers are! You would not write to each other but upon the most urgent necessity in the world; and when obliged to take up a pen to say that such a horse is ill, or such a relation dead, it is done in the fewest possible words.

MANSFIELD PARK

AUNTS

—

On Aunthood

Now that you are become an Aunt, you are a person of some consequence and must excite great interest whatever you do. I have always maintained the importance of Aunts as much as possible.

LETTER TO HER NIECE CAROLINE

On the Joys of Aunthood as Opposed to Motherhood

I shall be very well off with all the children of a sister I love so much, to care about. There will be enough of them, in all probability, to supply every sort of sensation that declining life can need. There will be enough for every hope and every fear; and though my attachment to none can equal that of a parent, it suits my ideas of comfort better than what is warmer and blinder. My nephews and nieces! I shall often have a niece with me.

EMMA

CHILDREN

On Children as Conversation Pieces

On every formal visit a child ought to be one of the party, by way of provision for discourse. In the present case it took up to ten minutes to determine whether the boy were most like his father or mother, and in what particular he resembled either, for of course everybody differed, and everybody was astonished at the opinion of the others.

SENSE AND SENSIBILITY

On Greeting a New Baby

I give you joy of our new nephew, and hope if he ever
comes to be hanged it will not be till we are too old to
care about it.

LETTER TO HER SISTER CASSANDRA

On Loving Kids Even Though They're Kids

. . . though the children are sometimes very noisy and not
under such order as they ought and easily might, I cannot
help liking them and even loving them, which I hope may
not be wholly inexcusable in their and your affectionate aunt.

LETTER TO HER NIECE CAROLINE

47

On Hearing the News of a New Bundle of Joy

Poor woman! How can she honestly be breeding again?

LETTER TO HER SISTER CASSANDRA

On Well-behaved Children Being a Splendid Thing Indeed

I confess . . . I never think of time and quiet children with
any abhorrence.

SENSE AND SENSIBILITY

On a Surefire Method of Family Planning

I would recommend to her and Mr. D. the simple regimen of separate rooms.

LETTER TO HER SISTER CASSANDRA

WORLDLY THINGS

*A large income is the best recipe for happiness
I have ever heard of.*

MANSFIELD PARK

Money, or the lack of it, looms large in Jane Austen's novels. Both men and women make no secret of the fact that, if they lack money themselves, they must marry for it. The poet W. H. Auden wrote about Jane Austen's candid treatment of the subject:

> You could not shock her more than she shocks me;
> Beside her Joyce seems innocent as grass
> It makes me most uncomfortable to see
> An English spinster of the middle class
> Describe the amorous effects of "brass"
> Reveal so frankly and with such sobriety
> The economic basis of society.

The economic facts of life were particularly grim for women. Estates always passed to the eldest male, and a woman could never inherit an estate, not even from her husband. A woman would have a dowry, but it would become her husband's property upon marriage. The wife's lawyers would negotiate the amount of her "pin money" or personal allowance, and a woman might receive a jointure, a large piece of property with which to support herself after her husband died.

*The only real currency a woman possessed was her looks
and charm and their power to catch a husband. And if she
didn't marry, she would still need that charm to endear her
to the extended family that she would count on to support
her. A flattering tongue would also help in this regard, but
one can hardly blame Jane, caught in this harsh reality, to
exercise her poison pen on occasion.*

MONEY

—

On What Money Doesn't Buy

Money can only give happiness when there is nothing
else to give it.

SENSE AND SENSIBILITY

On Why Donald Trump's Book Sold

. . . the rich are always respectable, whatever be their
style of writing.

THE LETTERS OF JANE AUSTEN

On Money and Happiness

What have wealth and grandeur to do with happiness?
Grandeur has but little . . . but wealth has much to do
with it.

SENSE AND SENSIBILITY

On the Bottom Line

Everything is to be got with money.

MANSFIELD PARK

LOOKS

—

On Beauty vs. Brains

. . . she is, in fact, a beautiful girl . . . and till it appears
that men are much more philosophic on the subject of
beauty than they are generally supposed, till they do fall
in love with well informed minds instead of handsome
faces, a girl, with such loveliness . . . has a certainty of
being admired and sought after.

EMMA

On Beauty vs. Brains Part Two

. . . notwithstanding your forbidding squint, your greasy tresses, and your swelling back, which are more frightful than imagination or paint or pen describe, I cannot refrain from expressing my raptures at the engaging qualities of your mind, which so amply atone for the horror with which your first appearance must ever inspire the unwary visitor.

THE JUVENILIA OF JANE AUSTEN

On Growing Old Gracelessly

There is something very trying to a young woman who has been a beauty in the loss of her personal attractions.

SENSE AND SENSIBILITY

On Never Judging People by Appearances

Varnish and gilding hide many stains.

MANSFIELD PARK

On Weight Loss

> I am going to have my dinner
> After which I shan't be thinner.

THE JUVENILIA OF JANE AUSTEN

FLATTERY

—

On the Timeless Skill of Sucking Up . . .

> It is happy for you that you possess the talent of flattering
> with delicacy. May I ask whether these pleasing attentions
> proceed from the impulse of the moment, or are the result
> of previous study?

PRIDE AND PREJUDICE

. . . And Why You Should Never Fall for It . . .

> What one means one day, you know, one may not mean
> the next.

NORTHANGER ABBEY

. . . And Why You Always Do

. . . it requires uncommon steadiness of reason to resist
the attraction of being called the most charming girl in the
world.

NORTHANGER ABBEY

On a Backhanded Compliment . . .

I should not be surprised if you were thought one of the
prettiest girls in the room, there is a great deal in novelty.

LADY SUSAN

. . . And Yet Another Backhanded Compliment

A lucky contraction of brow has rescued her countenance
from the disgrace of insipidity, by giving it the strong
characters of pride and ill nature.

SENSE AND SENSIBILITY

55

JANE'S POISON PEN

On Being a Bit of a Curmudgeon

... it is my unhappy fate seldom to treat people so well as they deserve.

THE LETTERS OF JANE AUSTEN

Jane at Her Bitchiest, on the Horrors of War ...

How horrible it is to have so many people killed! And what a blessing that one cares for none of them!

THE LETTERS OF JANE AUSTEN

... Jane at Her Very Bitchiest ...

(She) was brought to bed yesterday of a dead child, some weeks before she expected, owing to fright. I suppose she happened unawares to look at her husband.

THE LETTERS OF JANE AUSTEN

. . . On Trying Not to Be So Cranky . . .

Incline us oh God! to think humbly of ourselves, to
deserve only in the examination of our own conduct, to
consider our fellow creatures with kindness.

THE LETTERS OF JANE AUSTEN

. . . But Still Needing to Be a Little Cranky

I do not want people to be very agreeable, as it saves me
the trouble of liking them a great deal.

THE LETTERS OF JANE AUSTEN

On "Stop Me Before I Insult Again"

But if I go on, I shall displease you by saying what I think of persons you esteem. Stop me whilst you can.

PRIDE AND PREJUDICE

On Being an Advocate for Good Oral Hygiene

I was as civil to them as their bad breath would allow me.

LETTER TO CASSANDRA

On Faking It

. . . her illnesses never occurred but for her own convenience.

EMMA

On Hoping Her Brother Will Not Obtain a Membership in the Hair Club for Men

God bless you. I hope you continue beautiful and brush your hair, but not all off.

LETTER TO HER BROTHER FRANK

On Annoying Women

Insufferable woman! . . . Worse than I had supposed.
Absolutely insufferable! A little upstart, vulgar, being . . .
and all her air of pert pretension and under bred finery.

EMMA

On Putting Down an Unpleasant Woman

She is a large, ungenteel woman, with self-satisfied and
would-be elegant manners . . .

LETTER TO CASSANDRA

. . . And Feeling Bad About it Later

After have much praised or much blamed anybody, one is
generally sensible of something just the reverse soon
afterwards.

LETTER TO CASSANDRA

On Being a Tough Cookie

There is a stubbornness about me that can never bear to
be frightened at the will of others. My courage always
rises with every attempt to intimidate me.

PRIDE AND PREJUDICE

WORLDLY THINGS

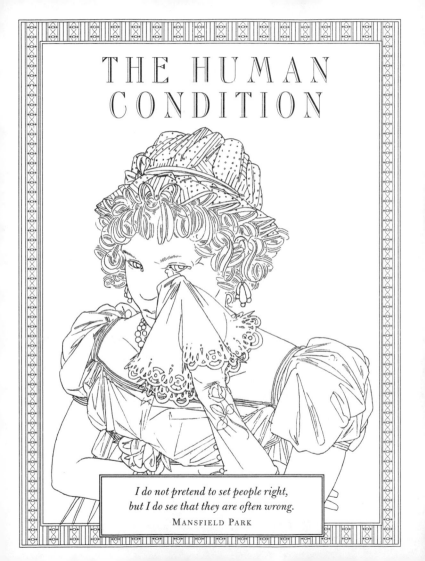

THE HUMAN CONDITION

I do not pretend to set people right,
but I do see that they are often wrong.
MANSFIELD PARK

The genius of Jane Austen's work was her close observation of human nature. There are few real villains or shining heroes in her books, only complete characters with their own specific set of foibles, people neither all good nor all bad.

She was scrupulous about writing only what she knew, and what she knew was how well-brought-up people behaved in social situations. One critic has speculated that this is why none of her books contains scenes of men conversing alone, with no women present; since she couldn't observe herself what such a conversation would be like, she wouldn't write it. Another critic (okay, it's really one of us) adds that this also might explain why all Austen's romantic endings are written in the third person narrative and often quickly concluded. Since Jane never had a satisfying denouement of that kind herself, perhaps it was another kind of conversation she didn't feel she could invent.

VICES AND VIRTUES
—

On Men Prizing Speed over Artistry, in All Things

The power of doing anything with quickness is always much prized by the possessor, and often without any attention to the imperfection of the performance.

PRIDE AND PREJUDICE

On Idle Men

A man who has nothing to do with his own time has no conscience in his intrusion on that of others.

SENSE AND SENSIBILITY

On Being a Psychic Friend

And have you never known the pleasure and triumph of a lucky guess? I pity you. I thought you cleverer, for depend upon it, a lucky guess is never merely luck. There is always some talent in it.

EMMA

63

On Ricki Lake et al.

Her kindness is not sympathy; her good nature is not ten-
derness. All that she wants is gossip, and she only likes
me now because I supply it.

SENSE AND SENSIBILITY

On False Modesty

Nothing is more deceitful . . . than the appearance of humility. It is often only pride and carelessness of opinion, and sometimes an indirect boast.

PRIDE AND PREJUDICE

On an Easily Granted Wish

I have no wish to be distinguished; and I have every reason to hope I never shall. Thank heaven I cannot be forced into genius and eloquence.

SENSE AND SENSIBILITY

65

On One Man's Meat Being Another's Poison

His own stomach could bear nothing rich, and he could never believe other people to be different from himself. What was unwholesome to him he regarded as unfit for anybody.

EMMA

On the Heat of the Moment

. . . angry people are not always wise.

PRIDE AND PREJUDICE

THE HUMAN CONDITION

On Jealousy

What wild imagination one forms, where dear self is concerned! How sure to be mistaken!

PERSUASION

On Trying Not to Be Jealous

(I am) as glad as I can be at anybody's being rich except you and me.

LETTER TO HER SISTER CASSANDRA

On Prejudice

. . . Where there is a disposition to dislike, a motive will never be wanting . . .

LADY SUSAN

On Phoniness

She professed a love of books without reading, was lively without wit, and generally good humored without merit.

THE JUVENILIA OF JANE AUSTEN

On Everyone Having Their Faults

There is, I believe, in every disposition a tendency to some particular evil, a natural defect, which not even the best education can overcome.

PRIDE AND PREJUDICE

On Hype

I set him down as sensible, rather than brilliant. There is nobody brilliant nowadays.

LETTER TO HER SISTER CASSANDRA

PESSIMISM AND OPTIMISM
—

On the Importance of Self-Pampering

I always deserve the best treatment, because I never put up with any other.

EMMA

On Being in a Dark Mood

. . . it is a vile world, we are all for self and I expected no
better for any of us.

LETTER TO HER NIECE CAROLINE

On Being in a Really Really Good Mood

I am certainly the most fortunate creature that ever existed!

PRIDE AND PREJUDICE

On Being in a Really Really Bad Mood

Misery such as mine has no pride. I care not who knows
that I am wretched . . . those who suffer little may be
proud and independent as they like, may resist or return
mortification, but I cannot. I must feel, I must be
wretched, and they are welcome to enjoy the conscious-
ness of it that can . . . But to appear happy when I am so
miserable—Oh! Who can require it?

SENSE AND SENSIBILITY

SELFISHNESS

—

On Selfishness

(She was) one of those persons who think nothing can be dangerous or difficult, or fatiguing, to anybody but themselves.

MANSFIELD PARK

On Being Able to Own Up to Selfishness

I have been a selfish being all my life, in practice, though not in principle.

PRIDE AND PREJUDICE

SELF-KNOWLEDGE

—

On Self-Delusion

Where so many hours have been spent in convincing myself that I am right, is there not some reason to fear I may be wrong?

SENSE AND SENSIBILITY

On the Timeless Appeal of Mumbling

I cannot speak well enough to be unintelligible.

NORTHANGER ABBEY

ON HAPPINESS AND UNHAPPINESS

—

On Happiness

I would much rather have been merry than wise.

EMMA

On the Dismal Ineffectiveness of Whining

I never heard that even Queen Mary's Lamentation did her any good, and I could not therefore expect benefit from mine.

THE LETTERS OF JANE AUSTEN

On "I Did It My Way"

I wish as well as everybody else to be perfectly happy but like everybody else it must be in my own way.

SENSE AND SENSIBILITY

On a Truly Good Inheritance

I have the honor . . . and the advantage of inheriting a disposition to hope for good, which no inheritance of houses or lands can ever equal the value of.

EMMA

On Disagreeable Tasks

Nothing ever fatigues me, but doing what I do not like.

MANSFIELD PARK

On Good Times

Perfect happiness, even in memory, is not common.

EMMA

On How to Treat Those Who Have Done One Wrong

You ought certainly to forgive them as a Christian, but never to admit them in your sight, or allow their names to be mentioned in your hearing.

PRIDE AND PREJUDICE

On Carpe Diem

Why not seize the pleasure at once? How often is happiness destroyed by preparation, foolish preparation?

EMMA

On Suffering

My sore throats are always worse than anyone's.

PERSUASION

On Persistence

. . . if one scheme of happiness fails, human nature turns to another; if the first calculation is wrong we make a second better, we find comfort somewhere.

MANSFIELD PARK

On Being Sensitive

My good opinion once lost is lost forever.

PRIDE AND PREJUDICE

On Enjoying the Here and Now . . .

> . . . our pleasures in this world are always to be paid for,
> and that we often purchase them at a great disadvantage,
> giving ready-monied actual happiness for a draft on the
> future, that may not be honored.

PRIDE AND PREJUDICE

. . . But Accepting the Inevitability of Bad Luck . . .

> None of us expects to be in smooth water all our days.

PERSUASION

. . . And Then Accepting the Inevitability of Good Luck

> I must endeavor to subdue my mind to my fortune. I must
> learn to brook being happier than I deserve.

PERSUASION

YOUTH AND AGE

—

On the Positive Attributes of Growing Older

By the by, as I must leave off being young, I find many douceurs in being a sort of chaperone (at dances), for I am put on the sofa near the fire and can drink as much wine as I like.

LETTER TO HER SISTER CASSANDRA

On the Folly of Youth

There is something so amiable in the prejudices of a young mind, that one is sorry to see them give way to the reception of more general opinions.

SENSE AND SENSIBILITY

On Things Could Be Worse . . .

She considered that there were misfortunes of a much greater magnitude than the loss of a ball experienced every day by some part of mortality, and that the time might come when she would herself look back with wonder and perhaps envy on her having known no greater vexation.

THE JUVENILIA OF JANE AUSTEN

. . . And They Will Be

Every generation has its improvements.

MANSFIELD PARK

75

WIT AND HUMOR

—

On Making Fun of Those Who Deserve It

I dearly love a laugh . . . but . . . I hope I never ridicule what is wise or good. Follies and nonsense, whims and inconsistencies do divert me, I own, and I laugh at them whenever I can.

PRIDE AND PREJUDICE

On Whether It Is Better to Be Smart, or Funny

Wisdom is better than wit, and in the long run will certainly have the laugh on her side.

LETTER TO HER NIECE FANNY

On the Inadvisability of Using Pension Funds as a Topic for Convention Humor

An annuity is a very serious business.

SENSE AND SENSIBILITY

On the Cruelty of Comedians

The wisest and best of men, nay the wisest and best of their actions may be rendered ridiculous by a person whose first object in life is a joke

PRIDE AND PREJUDICE

ADVICE: GIVING IT AND RECEIVING IT
—

On Advice

. . . advice is only good or bad as the event decides.

PERSUASION

On Taking All Advice, Including Jane's, with a Giant Lump of Salt

We all love to instruct, though we can only teach what is not worth knowing.

PRIDE AND PREJUDICE

On the Pot Calling the Kettle You Know What

Nor could she help fearing, on more serious, that, like many other great moralists and preachers she had been eloquent on a point in which her own conduct would ill bear examination.

PERSUASION

On the Conventional Wisdom

. . . where an opinion is general, it is usually correct.

MANSFIELD PARK

78

SOCIAL LIFE

For what do we live, but to make sport for our neighbors,
and laugh at them in our turn?

PRIDE AND PREJUDICE

In the world of a Jane Austen novel, nobody ever seems to have a job. This is actually a fairly accurate representation of the middle class in her time. The aristocracy in England was on the wane toward the end of the eighteenth century. Both the French and the American revolutions were happening, and the Industrial Revolution was coming on fast. Also, the aristocrats had been multiplying for many generations and it was getting to the point where all of them could not have their own private ten thousand acres and a mansion. England isn't that big of a country.

But the middle class gentry, which was the only class Jane wrote about, was not a bad place to be. If you had a little land, say a thousand acres, and a not-too-taxing position in the clergy or military, you still had plenty of time to dance, play cards, go visiting, and gossip with your neighbors. Modern readers are usually a little taken aback when the Dashwoods, reduced to what they seem to think of as dire poverty, have to suddenly make do with only three servants. So England was a good place to be at this time, unless of course you were one of those servants, in which case you had a whole other set of problems (*see* Charles Dickens' Little Advice Book).

The fashions of the time were not the body-concealing crinolines and corsets you sometimes see in old movie adaptations of Austen novels. The dresses were actually quite revealing, usually thin muslin, often white, with plunging necklines and only a thin chemise worn underneath. The racier girls would sometimes damp down the chemises with water to make them more form-fitting, creating a sort of nineteenth-century version of the Wet T-shirt contest. Come to think of it, this may be why women were considered over the hill in their mid-twenties.

FASHION

—

On Why Men Never Notice One's New Dress

It would be mortifying to the feelings of many ladies, could they be made to understand how little the heart of man is affected by what is costly or new in their attire . . . Woman is fine for her own satisfaction . . .

NORTHANGER ABBEY

On Picking a Hat

I cannot help thinking that it is more natural to have flowers grow out of the head than fruit.

LETTER TO HER SISTER CASSANDRA

On Convertibles Being a Menace to Good Grooming

Open carriages are nasty things. A clean gown is not five minutes wear in them. You are splashed getting in and getting out; and the wind takes your hair and your bonnet in every direction.

NORTHANGER ABBEY

On Never Letting Them See You Sweat

What dreadful hot weather we have! It keeps me in a continual state of inelegance.

LETTER TO HER SISTER CASSANDRA

On Evening Clothes

Mrs. Powlett was at once expensively and nakedly dressed.

LETTER TO HER SISTER CASSANDRA

On Having a Bad Face Day

Morning visits are never fair by women at her time of life, who make themselves up so little.

PERSUASION

On Having Nothing to Wear

I am determined to buy a handsome new (gown) whenever I can, and I am so tired and ashamed of half my present stock that I even blush at the sight of the wardrobe which contains them.

LETTER TO HER SISTER CASSANDRA

GOSSIP

On Gossip

Which of my all important nothings should I tell you first?

LETTER TO HER SISTER CASSANDRA

On Making a Good Impression

You are never sure of a good impression being durable.
Everybody must sway it.

PERSUASION

On Men Being Bigger Gossips

You men have such restless curiosity! Talk of the curiosity
of women, indeed! Tis nothing.

NORTHANGER ABBEY

On Being Gossip-Worthy

Human nature is so well disposed toward those in interesting situations, that a young person who either marries
or dies, is sure to be kindly spoken of.

EMMA

On Talking Behind One's Back

Abuse everybody but me.

THE LETTERS OF JANE AUSTEN

84

THE SOCIAL WHIRL:

—

Pro...

On Being a Party Girl

One cannot have too large a party.

EMMA

On Leaving Them Wanting More

It was a delightful visit—perfect, in being much too short.

EMMA

On Being a Wet Blanket

I am afraid that the pleasantness of an employment does not always evince its propriety.

SENSE AND SENSIBILITY

On the Occasional Necessity of Getting the Heck Out of Dodge

. . if the adventures will not befall a young lady in her own village. She must seek them abroad.

NORTHANGER ABBEY

On Silence While Traveling

We . . . were exceedingly agreeable, as we did not speak above once in three miles.

THE LETTERS OF JANE AUSTEN

. . . And Con

On the Thrill of the Social Whirl

The sooner every party breaks up the better.

EMMA

On Thinking You Look Great on the Dance Floor

Fine dancing, I believe, like virtue, must be its own reward. Those who are standing by are usually thinking of something very different.

EMMA

On the Wisdom of Remaining a Couch Potato

The folly of people's not staying comfortably at home when they can! . . . five dull hours in another man's house, with nothing to say or to hear that was not said

and heard yesterday, and may not be said and heard again
tomorrow . . . colder rooms and worse company than
they might have had at home.

EMMA

On How to Stop the Conversation Cold

From politics, it was an easy step to silence.

NORTHANGER ABBEY

On How to Get Along with Fools

Elinor agreed with it all, for
she did not think he
deserved the compliment of
rational opposition.

SENSE AND
SENSIBILITY

HOME LIFE

—

On Housekeeping

I am a very good housekeeper. which I have no reluctance
in doing, because I really think it is my peculiar excellence, and for this reason, I always take care to provide
such things as please my own appetite, which I consider
as the chief merit in housekeeping.

LETTER TO HER SISTER CASSANDRA

On There Being No Place Like Home

One does not love a place the less for having suffered
in it.

PERSUASION

...AND SERVANTS

—

On an Entourage Being a Somewhat Draining Thing

And I do believe those are best off, that have fewest
servants.

LADY SUSAN

88

. . . for in these great places the gardeners are the only people who can go where they like.

MANSFIELD PARK

THE COUNTRY

—

Pro . . .

On Nature Being the Best Refreshment

To sit in the shade on a fine day and look upon verdure is the most perfect refreshment.

MANSFIELD PARK

89

On the Joys of Nature

When I look out on such a night as this, I feel as if there could be neither wickedness nor sorrow in the world; and there certainly would be less of both if the sublimity of nature were more attended to, and people were more carried out of themselves by contemplating such a scene.

MANSFIELD PARK

...And Con

On the Dullness of Country Life

One day in the country is exactly like another.

NORTHANGER ABBEY

On Sex

I assure you there is as much of that going in the country as in town!

PRIDE AND PREJUDICE

...AND THE CITY

On Urban Life

We do not look in great cities for our best morality.

MANSFIELD PARK

THE PROFESSIONS

On a Certain Profession

Go into the law! With as much ease as I was told to go into this wilderness.

MANSFIELD PARK

On the Life of a Clergyman Being an Easy Gig

A clergyman has nothing to do but be slovenly and self-ish, read the newspaper, watch the weather, and quarrel with his wife. His curate does all the work, and the business of his own life is to dine.

MANSFIELD PARK

On the Joys of Unemployment

I have long been convinced, though every profession is necessary and honorable in its turn, it is only the lot of those who are not obliged to follow any, who can live in a regular way.

PERSUASION

FRIENDSHIP

—

On Having Friends in Low Places

I have frequently thought that I must be intended by
nature to be fond of low company. I am so little at ease
among strangers of gentility!

SENSE AND SENSIBILITY

*On Why You Shouldn't Dump Your Girlfriend When You Get
a Boyfriend*

Friendship is the finest balm for the pangs of despised
love.

NORTHANGER ABBEY

On Being Choosy . . .

. . . let me have only the company of the people I love, let
me only be where I like and with whom I like, and the
devil take the rest, say I.

NORTHANGER ABBEY

. . . And Whom to Choose

> My idea of good company . . . is the company of clever,
> well-informed people, who have a great deal of conversa-
> tion; that is what I call good company

PERSUASION

THE WORLD

—

On the Big, Big Picture

> . . . the welfare of every nation depends upon the virtue
> of its individuals, and any one who offends in so gross a
> manner against decorum and propriety is certainly has-
> tening its ruin.

THE JUVENILIA OF JANE AUSTEN

93

THE LITERARY LIFE

Where . . . did you pick up this unmeaning gibberish . . . ?
You have been studying novels I suspect.

JUVENILIA

Jane Austen started her life as an author at the tender age of twelve. Her first book was a parody of romantic novels entitled "Love and Friendship," and for the rest of her life, she remained both a prolific novelist and an uncertain speller.

It is said that she wrote in the mornings, after playing the piano, in a room with a purposely squeaky-hinged door, so she could hear anyone approaching. She wrote on a small piece of paper which she would secrete under her blotter. Her first novel to be sold, Northanger Abbey, only earned her ten pounds, and it languished unpublished for years until she bought it back. Her first published novel, Sense and Sensibility, was printed with her own money (borrowed from her brother Henry); fortunately it was sold well, and her second novel, Pride and Prejudice, was printed at the publishers' expense. Even though her books were popular, Jane only earned about seven hundred pounds in her lifetime from her writing. We got more than that for just picking quotes out of her books, and we're feeling pretty guilty about it. However, not guilty enough to give her descendants any of the money, so don't call.

Novel-reading was not considered a respectable leisure time activity in Jane Austen's day. It was looked on much as television-viewing is today: as a waste of time for trivial people in search of sensationalistic entertainment. People probably lied about not reading novels the same way they lie now about not watching TV.

Letter-writing was mostly businesslike. Since the recipient always paid the postage, an overly-long social letter was about as welcome as an overly-long collect call is now. Luckily, this did not stop Jane from writing letters, because it is from these letters we get the clearest picture of her real views on many subjects. But unfortunately, after Jane's death, Cassandra burned most of her letters and cut portions out of others. Apparently Jane Austen's family did not want posterity to know what a wicked tongue she truly had.

WRITING

—

On the Overwriting of Others

I am always afraid of finding a clever novel too clever.

LETTER TO HER SISTER CASSANDRA

On a Rival

Walter Scott has no business to write novels, especially good ones. It is not fair. He has fame and profit enough as a poet, and should not be taking the bread out of other people's mouths. I do not like him and do not mean to like "Waverly" if I can help it, but I fear I must . . . I have made up my mind to like no novels really, but Miss Edgeworth's, yours and my own.

LETTER TO HER NIECE ANNA

On Being a Perfectionist

. . . but an artist cannot do anything slovenly.

LETTER TO HER SISTER CASSANDRA

On the Importance of Rewrites

I hope when you have written a great deal more you will be equal to scratching out some of the past.

LETTER TO HER NIECE ANNA

98

On Taking Autobiographies with a Grain of Salt

Those who tell their own story . . . must be listened to
with caution.

SANDITON

On Why Good Writing Is Important

I declare after all there is no enjoyment like reading! How
much sooner one tires of anything than of book!

PRIDE AND PREJUDICE

On Another Writer

Shakespeare one gets acquainted with
without knowing how. It is part of an
Englishman's constitution. His
thoughts and beauties are so spread
abroad that one touches them everywhere,
one is intimate with him by instinct.

MANSFIELD PARK

On Why Happy Endings Are Best

A heroine returning, at the close of her career, to her native village, all in the triumph of recovered reputation and all the dignity of a countess . . . is an event on which the pen of the contriver may well delight to dwell; it gives credit to every conclusion, and the author must share in the glory she so liberally bestows.

NORTHANGER ABBEY

On Not Wanting It to End

. . . but for my own part, if a book is well written, I always find it too short.

THE JUVENILIA OF JANE AUSTEN

NOVELS

—

On Novels

The person, be it gentleman or lady, who has not pleasure in a good novel, must be intolerably stupid.

NORTHANGER ABBEY

On People Who Put Down Novels . . .

Only a novel . . . in short, only some work in which the
most thought and knowledge of human nature, the happi-
est delineation of varieties, the liveliest effusions of wit
and humor are conveyed to the world in the best chosen
language.

NORTHANGER ABBEY

. . . And on What Novelists Would Like to Do to Those People

Let us leave it to the reviewers to abuse such effusions of
fancy at their leisure, and over every new novel to talk in
threadbare strains of the trash with which the press now
groans. Let us not desert one another; we are an injured
body. Although our (novels) have afforded more extensive
and unaffected pleasure than those of any other literary
corporation in the world, no species of composition has
been so much decried. From pride, ignorance, or fashion,
our foes are almost as many as our readers.

NORTHANGER ABBEY

101

HER OWN WRITING

—

On Being Her Own Worst Critic

I think I may boast myself to be, with all possible vanity, the most unlearned and uninformed female who ever dared to be an authoress.

LETTER TO THE PRINCE OF WALES' LIBRARIAN

On Having a Bad Day Writing

I do not know what is the matter with me today, but I cannot write quietly; I am always wandering away into some exclamation or other. Fortunately I have nothing very particular to say.

LETTER TO HER SISTER CASSANDRA

On Her Own Writing, and Being Far Too Modest in the Bargain

The little bit (two inches wide) of ivory on which I work with so fine a brush as produces little effect after much labor.

LETTER TO HER SISTER CASSANDRA

On the Superiority of Her Own Readers

I could not preach, but to the educated.

MANSFIELD PARK

On Knowing Your Topic . . .

Let other pens dwell on guilt and misery.

MANSFIELD PARK

. . . And Assuming Her Audience Is Very Clever Indeed

I do not write for such elves
As have not a great deal of ingenuity themselves.

LETTER TO HER SISTER CASSANDRA

On How Much Her Books Meant to Her

I can no more forget it (SENSE AND SENSIBILITY) than a
mother can forget her sucking child.

THE LETTERS OF JANE AUSTEN

103

On the Cure for Writer's Block

(I am) not at all in a humor for writing; I must write on till I am.

LETTER TO HER SISTER CASSANDRA

On the Virtue of Simplicity

(I) believe that I have not yet, as almost every writer of fancy does sooner or later, overwritten myself.

LETTER TO HER SISTER CASSANDRA

On Why Jane Could Never Write a Harlequin Romance

I could not sit seriously down to write a serious romance under any other motive than to save my life; and if it were indispensable for me to keep it up and never relax into laughing at myself or other people, I am sure I should be hung before I finished the first chapter. No, I must keep to my own style and go on in my own way; and though I may never succeed again in that, I am convinced that I should totally fail in any other.

LETTER TO THE PRINCE OF WALES' LIBRARIAN

On the Godlike Power of Writing

The weather is mended, which I attribute to my writing about it.

LETTER TO CASSANDRA

POETRY

On a Sure-fire Romance Killer

I wonder who first discovered the efficacy of poetry in driving away love! . . . if it be only a slight, thin sort of inclination, I am convinced that one good sonnet will starve it entirely away.

PRIDE AND PREJUDICE

On Those Who Take Poetry Too Seriously . . .

. . . it was the misfortune of poetry, to be seldom safely enjoyed by those who enjoyed it completely, and that the strong feelings which alone could estimate it truly, were the very feelings which ought to taste it but sparingly.

PERSUASION

. . . And Something Polite to Say to Them

It is not everybody who has your passion for dead leaves.

SENSE AND SENSIBILITY

LETTER WRITING

—

On Writing Letters for the Fun of It . . .

I am very much flattered by your commendation of my
last letter, for I write only for fame, and without any view
to pecuniary emolument.

. . . And When It's Not So Fun . . .

How ill I have written. I begin to hate myself.

THE LETTERS OF JANE AUSTEN

. . . And Even Downright Dangerous . . .

I may now finish my letter and go and hang myself, for I
am sure I can neither write nor do anything which will
not appear insipid to you.

THE LETTERS OF JANE AUSTEN

. . . And When You Don't Even Want to Get the Damn Things

The post office has a great charm at one period in our lives. When you have lived to my age, you will begin to think letters are never worth going through the rain for.

THE LETTERS OF JANE AUSTEN

BAD WRITING

—

On Purple Prose

. . . that expression of 'violently in love' is so hackneyed, so doubtful, so indefinite . . . It is as often applied to feelings which arise from an half-hour's acquaintance, as to a real, strong attachment.

PRIDE AND PREJUDICE

On Characters Too Good to Be True

. . . pictures of perfection as you know make me sick and wicked.

LETTER TO HER NIECE FANNY

On Clichés

I abhor every commonplace phrase by which wit is
intended; and 'setting one's cap at a man,' or 'making a con-
quest' are the most odious of all. Their tendency is gross
and illiberal; and if their construction could ever be deemed
clever, time has long ago destroyed all its ingenuity.

SENSE AND SENSIBILITY

On Not Wasting Your Time

You may as well take back that tiresome book she would
lend me and pretend I have read it through. I really cannot be plaguing myself for ever with all the new poems
and states of the nation that come out.

PERSUASION

On Books She Hates and Books She Loves—or—
Jane Just Goes Off

I am no indiscriminate novel reader. The mere trash of
the common circulating library, I hold in the highest contempt. You will never hear me advocating those puerile
emanations which detail nothing but discordant princi-
ples incapable of amalgamation, or those vapid tissues of
ordinary occurrences from which no useful deductions

can be drawn. In vain may we put them into a literary alembid; we distill nothing which can add to science. You understand me I am sure? . . . The novels which I approve are such as display human nature with grandeur, such as show her in the sublimities of intense feeling, such as exhibit the progress of strong passion from the first germ of incipient susceptibility to the utmost energies of reason half-dethroned, where we see the strong spark of woman's captivations elicit such fire in the soul of man as leads him, hazard all, dare all, achieve all, to obtain her. Such are the works I peruse with delight, I hope I may say, with amelioration. They hold forth the most splendid portraitures of high conceptions, unbounded views, illimitable ardor, indomitable decision, and even when the event is mainly anti-prosperous to the high toned machinations of the prime character, the potent, pervading hero of the story, it leaves us full of generous emotions for him; our hearts are paralyzed.

SANDITON

ODD TOPICS

On an unorthodox definition of sobriety:

There is no drinking at Oxford now, I assure you. Nobody drinks there. You would hardly meet with a man who goes beyond his four pints at the utmost.

NORTHANGER ABBEY

Jane Austen was nothing if not opinionated. One odd topic she loved to hold forth on was the subject of wine, a subject that has been popular with writers throughout history.

Jane and her sister made their own mead, a kind of wine from fermented honey, and during her final illness, she expressed great concern that there was still enough money in the household to buy that honey.

Whatever her subject, what she has to say is bound to be intriguing . . .

WINE

—

On the Considerable Fun to Be Had Watching Drunks . . .

. . . (She) thought herself obliged . . . to run around the room after her drunken husband. His avoidance, and her pursuit, with the probable intoxication of both, was an amusing scene.

LETTER TO CASSANDRA

. . . And the Fun to Be Had Being One

Elinor, as she swallowed the chief of it, reflected though its good effects on a cholicky gout were, at present, of little importance, its healing powers on a disappointed heart might be as reasonably tried on herself as on her sister.

SENSE AND SENSIBILITY

On the Positive Effects of Alcohol . . .

The more wine I drink, in moderation, the better I am. I am always best of an evening.

. . . And the Negative

I believe I drank too much wine last night
. . . I know not how else to account
for the shaking of my hand today.

LETTER TO
HER SISTER CASSANDRA

DENTISTRY

—

On Dentistry . . .

I had rather undergo the greatest tortures in the world
than have a tooth drawn.

THE JUVENILIA OF JANE AUSTEN

. . . And Life Before Novocain

I wish there were no such things as teeth in the world; they
are nothing but plagues to one, and I dare say that people
might easily invent something to eat with instead of them.

THE JUVENILIA OF JANE AUSTEN

GOOD ADVICE IN GENERAL

—

On the Dangers of Passing Out

Beware of fainting fits . . . though at the time they may be
refreshing and agreeable, yet believe me they will, in the
end, if too often repeated and at improper seasons, prove
destructive to your constitution . . . Run mad as often as
you choose; but do not faint.

THE JUVENILIA OF JANE AUSTEN

On Why Surprise Parties Never Work

Surprises are foolish things. The pleasure is not
enhanced, and the inconvenience is often considerable.

EMMA

On Shopping Tips

. . . it is one of my maxims always to buy a good horse
when I meet with one.

NORTHANGER ABBEY

On the Necessity of Complaining

Those who do not complain are never pitied.

PRIDE AND PREJUDICE

On Nice Work If You Can Get It

No person . . . could be really in a state of secure and permanent health without spending at least six weeks by the
sea every year.

SANDITON

On Denial, as a Good Thing

It must be terrible for you to hear it talked of . . . I think the less that is said about such things, the better, the sooner 'tis blown over and forgot. And what good does talking ever do, you know?

SENSE AND SENSIBILITY

On Sour Grapes, as a Good Thing

I have often observed that resignation is never so perfect as when the blessing denied begins to lose somewhat of its value in our eyes.

PRIDE AND PREJUDICE

On Selective Memory, as a Good Thing

Think only of the past as its remembrance gives you pleasure.

PRIDE AND PREJUDICE

JANE PREDICTS THE FUTURE

I suppose all the World in sitting in Judgment upon the Princess of Wales . . . Poor woman, I shall support her as long as I can, because she is a Woman, and because I hate her husband . . . but if I must give up the Princess, I am resolved at least always to think that she would have been respectable, if the Prince had only behaved tolerably by her at first.

LETTER TO MARTHA LLOYD, 16 FEBRUARY 1813

Nearly all of Jane Austen's writings seem fresh to contemporary readers, but occasionally, one will come across a passage that is downright startling in its relevance. Sometimes it seems that Nostradamus has nothing on our Jane.

In the early nineteenth century, the Prince and Princess of Wales were behaving just as strangely as they do now. The Prince was the son of the often insane George III (the king the American colonies revolted against), so perhaps that's his excuse. His wife, the Princess of Wales, was beautiful, notorious for spending money, and much more popular than her husband the Prince, probably because she did not have a cellular phone. Their private warfare eventually became a large political problem. Both the Prince and the Princess had affairs openly, and if the BBC had existed then, they probably would have been on it talking about them. However, in the Prince Regent's defense, it should be noted that to the best of our historical knowledge, he never in his life expressed a desire to be a tampon.

MORE ON THE CURRENT ROYAL FAMILY...

—

On Prince Charles Wanting a Divorce Really Badly

I hear from Charles that he has written to Lord Spencer himself to be removed. I am afraid his Serene Highness will be in a passion and order some of our heads to be cut off.

THE LETTERS OF JANE AUSTEN

On Predicting the Sad State of Affairs for Miss Parker-Bowles

Camilla, good humored and merry and small,
For a husband, it happened, was at her last stake,
And having in vain danced at many a ball,
Is now very happy to jump at a wake.

LETTER TO HER DEAR FRIEND MARTHA LLOYD

119

On The Rest of The Royal Family

I do not know whether it ought to be so, but certainly silly things do cease to be silly if they are done by sensible people in an impudent way. Wickedness is always wickedness, but folly is not always folly.

EMMA

GENERAL PREDICTIONS

—

On Predicting the Popularity of Plastic Surgery

But people themselves alter so much, that there is something new to be observed in them for ever.

PRIDE AND PREJUDICE

On the Social Security Problem

People always live forever when there is any annuity to be paid them.

SENSE AND SENSIBILITY

On Predicting the Success of the TV Series E.R.

A sick chamber may often furnish the worth of volumes.

PERSUASION

On Predicting the Success of the Daytime Soap Opera Formula

Three or four families in a country village is the very thing to work on.

LETTER TO HER NIECE ANNA

On Not Worrying About the Ozone Layer

What fine weather this is . . . at least everybody fancies so, and imagination is everything.

THE LETTERS OF JANE AUSTEN

121

On Predicting the Success of Sharon Stone

(She) will never be easy till she has exposed herself in some public place.

PRIDE AND PREJUDICE

On What a Pity It Is Jane Austen Never Saw Emma Thompson

Simplicity, indeed, is beyond the reach of almost every actress by profession.

MANSFIELD PARK

On Predicting the Dialogue of Forrest Gump

Handsome is as handsome does, he is therefore a very ill-looking man.

LETTER TO HER SISTER CASSANDRA

On Predicting the United States Would Never Have National Health Care

What would we do with a doctor here? It would be only encouraging our servants and the poor to fancy themselves ill, if there was a doctor at hand.

LADY SUSAN

On O.J. Simpson

A new sort of way is this, for a young fellow to be making love, by breaking his mistress's head!

PERSUASION

On Predicting the Popularity of Sleazy Daytime Talk Shows

We live at home, quiet, confined, and our feelings prey upon us.

PERSUASION

On Predicting the Meteoric Rise of Rush Limbaugh

. . . if the judgment of Yahoos can ever be depended on, I suppose it may be now.

LETTER TO HER SISTER CASSANDRA

123

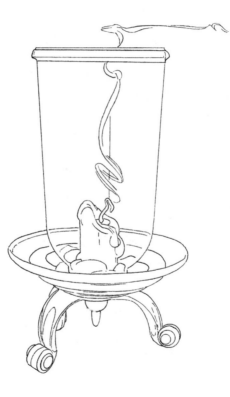

AND FINALLY...

—

Of All the Lines, in All Her Books, the Ones Jane Must Have Wished Had Been Spoken to Her

SHE: Now, be sincere; did you admire me for my impertinence?

HE: For the liveliness of your mind, I did.

PRIDE AND PREJUDICE

On Knowing When to End

You have delighted us long enough.

PRIDE AND PREJUDICE

BIBLIOGRAPHY

Julia Prewitt Brown, *A Reader's Guide to the Nineteenth-Century English Novel.* Macmillan, 1985.

W. A. Craik, *Jane Austen in Her Time.* Thomas Nelson and Sons, 1969.

John Halperin, *The Life of Jane Austen.* Johns Hopkins University Press, 1984.

Jane Aiken Hodge, *Only a Novel: The Double Life of Jane Austen.* Coward, McCann, and Geoghegan, 1972.

Marghanita Laski, *Jane Austen and Her World.* Charles Scribner's Sons, 1969.

Daniel Pool, *What Jane Austen Ate and Charles Dickens Knew.* Touchstone, 1993.

Fay Weldon, *Letters to Alice on First Reading Jane Austen.* Taplinger Publishing, 1985.

THE AUTHORS

Business, you know, may bring money, but friendship
hardly ever does.

EMMA

Cathryn Michon and Pamela Norris are two
gentlewomen of moderate means and
excellent tempers. Miss Michon lives in
the city and Miss Norris lives in the
country.

Note to Serious Jane Austen Scholars

If you have discovered any misquotations or historical inaccuracies in this book, please send them to:

Jane Austen's Little Bloopers
In care of **HarperCollins Publishers, Inc.**

There is undoubtedly an error or two in here; our proofreader caught several small ones before it was published. For example, her name was Jane and not Jean, and she lived in Bath (a town), not in the bath. The passage about how she stayed in there forever, to the consternation of her six brothers and sisters, has been deleted in this edition.

Thank you.